THIS BOOK BELONGS TO

....

KALLIE GEORGE

FLARE

ILLUSTRATED BY
GENEVIÈVE CÔTÉ

SIMPLY READ BOOKS

To my mom, for always giving me a shoulder to cry on. – K.G.

For Louise Rousseau, in the Universe. – G.C.

Published in 2014 by Simply Read Books
www.simplyreadbooks.com
Text © 2014 Kallie George
Illustrations © 2014 Geneviève Côté

Library and Archives Canada Cataloguing in Publication
George, K. (Kallie), 1983–, author
Flare / written by Kallie George ;
illustrated by Geneviève Côté.

ISBN 978-1-927018-50-7 (bound)

I. Côté, Geneviève, 1964–, illustrator II. Title.

PS8563.E6257F53 2014   jc813´.6   C2013-906051-0

We gratefully acknowledge for their financial support of our publishing program the Canada Council for the Arts, the BC Arts Council, and the Government of Canada through the Canada Book Fund (CBF).

Manufactured in Malaysia.

Book design by Naomi MacDougall.

10 9 8 7 6 5 4 3 2 1

CONTENTS

Flare Doesn't Cry

One day a tiny phoenix
was born.

There was a big flame.

Then a nest of ash.

In the nest, there was an egg.

Out of the egg hatched a
bird. A magical bird.

His feathers were soft
like the clouds,
strong like the wind,
and red and gold like the sun.

He sang,
"I am tough.
I am strong.
My name is Flare!"

Like all phoenixes, Flare
didn't have any parents.

High in the sky, Cloud
and Wind and Sun watched
over him.

Flare taught himself to
catch fish.

But when a fish got away,
he did not cry.

Flare taught himself to fly.

But when he fell, he did
not cry.

"It's okay to cry," said Sun.
"Crying can make you feel
better."

Flare shook his head.
"I am tough.
I am strong.
I do not cry," he sang.

Cloud and Wind and Sun
gathered in the sky.

"I don't think Flare knows
about crying," said Cloud.

"We must show him,"
said Wind.

"But we must be gentle,"
said Sun.

"Let me try first," said Cloud.

And off Cloud floated.

Cloud Cries

Cloud bobbed above Flare.

"Look at me," called Cloud.

Flare looked.

Cloud grew dark.
Cloud rumbled.

Rain fell.

Drip, drip, drip.

The drops landed on
Flare's beak.

"This is what tears feel like,"
Cloud said.

"Yuck! They are wet,"
said Flare.

He ducked under a tree.

"Crying is okay for clouds," said Flare. "But I will NEVER cry."

Cloud floated back to
Wind and Sun.

"It didn't work," said Cloud.

"That's all right," said Sun.

"Let me try next," said Wind.

And off Wind blew.

Wind Wails

Wind whooshed around Flare.

"Listen to me," said Wind.

Flare listened.

Wind wailed.

WAAAAH!

"This is what crying
sounds like," Wind howled.

"Yikes! I don't like that
sound," said Flare.

He ducked into
a cave.

"Crying is okay for
the wind," said Flare.
"But I will NEVER cry."

Wind blew back to
Cloud and Sun.

"It didn't work," said Wind.

"It's my turn next," said Sun.

"But what can you do?"
asked Cloud.

"You are bright and happy,"
said Wind.

"Crying is sad," said Cloud.

"Just watch," said Sun.

And off Sun blazed.

Sun Shows

Sun shone on Flare.

"Follow me," said Sun.

Sun lit up a path through the woods.

Flare followed.

The rays stopped beside
a big tree.

Flare stopped too.

A baby bird lay on the
ground.

It was crying.

"Be strong.
Be tough.
Don't cry," Flare sang
to the bird.

"I fell from my nest,"
cried the baby bird.
"My wing hurts!"

Flare looked.

The wing was bent
and broken.

"It hurts," cried the baby
bird. "It hurts. It hurts."

Flare felt sorry for the
baby bird.

He wanted to help.

But what could he do?

Flare's First Tears

Flare felt sadder and sadder.

Tears fell from his eyes.

Drip, drip, drip.

They splashed onto the baby bird's wing.

Flare cried... and cried.

When he was done,
he felt better.

So did the baby bird.

Much better!

"Thank you!" said the baby
bird. "You fixed my wing.
Your tears are magic. You
must be a phoenix."

"I *am* a phoenix!" said Flare.

And then he sang,
"I am tough.
I am strong.
And sometimes I cry!"

High in the sky, Cloud
and Wind and Sun nodded
proudly. And smiled.

THE END